RAINBOW magic ®

The Party Fairies

For Roisin and Alfie Starky-Oakley,
with love

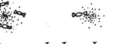

Special thanks to
Sue Mongredien

ORCHARD BOOKS
338 Euston Road, London NW1 3BH
Orchard Books Australia
Hachette Children's Books
Level 17/207 Kent Street, Sydney, NSW 2000
A Paperback Original
First published in Great Britain in 2005
Text © Working Partners Limited 2005
Created by Working Partners Limited, London W6 0QT
Illustrations © Georgie Ripper 2004
The right of Georgie Ripper to be identified as the illustrator
of this work has been asserted by her in accordance
with the Copyright, Designs and Patents Act, 1988.
A CIP catalogue record for this book is available
from the British Library.
ISBN 1 84362 821 X
10
Printed in Great Britain

Honey
the Sweet
Fairy

by Daisy Meadows

illustrated by Georgie Ripper

ORCHARD BOOKS

www.rainbowmagic.co.uk

Jack Frost's
Ice Castle

Forest
of
Greenwood

The Sweet
Shop

ne Park

Kirsty's
House

Charlotte's
House

Jamie Cooper's
House

A Very Special Party Invitation

Our gracious King and gentle Queen
Are loved by fairies all.
One thousand years have they ruled well,
Through troubles great and small.

In honour of their glorious reign
A party has been planned,
To celebrate their jubilee
Throughout all Fairyland.

The party is a royal surprise,
We hope they'll be delighted.
So shine your wand and press your dress...
For you have been invited!

RSVP: HRH THE FAIRY GODMOTHER

Contents

A Trip to the Sweet Shop

It was a lovely, sunny day, and Mr and Mrs Tate had set lunch outside in the garden. As Kirsty and her best friend, Rachel Walker, sat down to eat, Mrs Tate suddenly groaned aloud.

"I knew there was something else I meant to get from the shops this morning," she cried. "Gran's toffees!"

I promised I'd take her some this
evening, and I completely forgot to
buy them."

Kirsty put down her sandwich.
"Don't worry, Mum. We'll go to Mrs
Twist's Sweet Shop after lunch for
you," she suggested. She glanced at
Rachel. "What do you think?"

"Sure," Rachel said. "I've always got
time to go to the sweet shop!"

The two girls smiled at each other.

Rachel was staying with the Tates for a whole week. She and Kirsty had met one summer holiday, and they had been good friends ever since. Somehow, whenever the pair of them got together, they always seemed to have the most wonderful adventures. Fairy adventures!

"That reminds me," Mr Tate said. "I saw in the local newspaper that Mrs Twist is retiring. Her daughter's taking over the sweet shop from tomorrow. As this is her last day, Mrs Twist is throwing a party for all her customers." He winked at Kirsty and Rachel. "I read something about there being plenty of free sweets up for grabs, too!"

11

Kirsty nudged Rachel
at once. "Sweets
and a party,"
she repeated.
"How exciting!"
"We love parties,"
Rachel agreed, with a grin.

The two friends shared a secret.
They had been busy all week helping
the Party Fairies of Fairyland! The
fairies were preparing a surprise
celebration for the Fairy King and
Queen's 1000th jubilee — but wicked
Jack Frost had plans for his own rival
party. All week, he'd been sending his
goblins into the human world to
disrupt people's parties. Then,
whenever a Party Fairy zoomed in to
save the day, a goblin would try to

snatch her magical party bag and take it to Jack Frost.

Kirsty and Rachel had been helping the Party Fairies outwit the goblins, but they knew their work wasn't over yet. Not if Jack Frost had anything to do with it!

After lunch, Mrs Tate gave the girls some money for the toffees, and they set out for the sweet shop.

As they turned into the High Street, they saw that a few children were already clustered outside Mrs Twist's shop. But as they drew nearer, Kirsty and Rachel realised that something was wrong.

MRS. TWIST'S SWEET SHOP

OPEN

A boy was pulling a face as he licked a lollipop. And one little girl started to cry. "These sweeties taste funny," she wailed.

Kirsty and Rachel went into the shop, wondering what was going on. The tiny shop looked very festive. Colourful balloons hung from the ceiling, and party streamers were twined around the big jars of sweets that lined the shelves. Mrs Twist stood behind the counter as usual – but Kirsty noticed at once that she didn't look her normal cheerful self.

"Hello, Mrs Twist," Kirsty called. "Is everything all right?"

Mrs Twist shook her head sadly. "Not really," she replied. "It's my last day and I was hoping to have a wonderful party, but all my sweets are spoiled!"

A Sweet Surprise

As Kirsty and Rachel looked around, they could see what Mrs Twist meant. The pineapple chunks that she was trying to shake from their jar had become one big, sticky lump. The chocolate bars were soft and soggy as if they'd been lying in the sun. And the sherbet was fizzing so fiercely it made everyone sneeze!

Rachel nudged Kirsty. "Look!" she said in a low voice, pointing at one of the shelves.

Kirsty looked and saw a box of pink sugar mice, all with their paws over their eyes as if they were scared of something. The jelly babies looked worried too — they were all holding hands. And, to Kirsty's surprise, a group of jelly snakes in a jar were wriggling crossly and actually hissing!

She quickly pushed
the jar of snakes
to the back
of the shelf
before anyone
else noticed.

"Something very
weird is going on,"
Rachel whispered, as
the two friends heard
a low grumbling hum start
up from a jar of stripy humbugs.

Kirsty nodded. "It's got to be goblin
mischief!" she whispered back.

Mrs Twist put down the jar of pineapple
cubes, and pulled out a tray of chocolates
instead. Then she sighed in dismay.

"Oh, no! What's happened to these?"
Rachel and Kirsty went over to look.

19

The sweets had all melted on the tray, and right in the middle was a big hollow where something had pressed

into the soft chocolate. Rachel nudged Kirsty. She had immediately recognised the shape in the melted chocolate – it was a goblin footprint!

The girls exchanged glances and Kirsty promptly peered down at the floor. "If the goblin's got chocolate all over one foot..." she muttered to Rachel.

"...he'll have left footprints everywhere," Rachel added in a low voice. Then she pointed down at the floor. "Just like those!"

The girls quietly slipped away from the shop counter to follow the trail of chocolatey footprints. They seemed to lead to a door at the back of the shop.

"This is the door to Mrs Twist's stockroom," Kirsty whispered to her friend. "We can't just sneak in there without asking."

Rachel bit her lip. "Well, we can't just say, 'Excuse me, Mrs Twist, but we think there might be a goblin in your stockroom,' either. We'll—"

CRASH! Both girls jumped as they heard a loud noise from the other side of the door.

"Oh, no! It sounds like the goblin's wreaking havoc in there," Rachel hissed.

Before Kirsty could reply, she heard Mrs Twist saying, "This is no good. I can't give people these spoiled sweets. I'll get some new ones from the stockroom."

"No!" cried Kirsty hurriedly. She couldn't let Mrs Twist go in there – not with a sneaky goblin on the loose! "I mean, er…" she faltered, as Mrs Twist looked at her in suprise. "You can't leave the shop, Mrs Twist. Rachel and I will fetch the sweets for you."

Mrs Twist smiled. "Thank you, dear," she said gratefully. "Bring out anything you like the look of."

Kirsty nodded and cautiously pushed open the stockroom door. As both girls peeped into the room, they gasped in horror. Bottles and jars had been knocked over, and there were sweets scattered all across the floor. But, worst of all, there was a tiny fairy struggling desperately to hang

on to her magical party bag, as a grinning goblin fought to tug it out of her hands!

"It's Honey, the Sweet Fairy!" cried Kirsty. "And she's in trouble!"

Goblin Trouble

Kirsty and Rachel slipped inside the stockroom at once and shut the door behind them.

Honey was wearing a pale yellow dress and little sherbet-yellow shoes. Her golden-brown ponytail swung madly to and fro as she tried to save her party bag. "Oh, girls, please help me!"

she cried as she saw the friends.

"We certainly will," Rachel called back fiercely. Her gaze fell on a large jar of sweets. "Gobstoppers!" she exclaimed happily, unscrewing the lid. "Over here, Kirsty." Both girls took handfuls of the gobstoppers and began pelting the goblin with the hard, round sweets.

"Ouch!" yelped the goblin, as a gobstopper bounced off his long nose. He threw up his arms to protect his face – and let go of the party bag. But he released it so suddenly that Honey shot backwards into one of the shelves. All the breath was knocked out of her and she dropped her precious party bag!

"Oh, no!" gasped Honey, as the
shimmering golden fairy dust tumbled
out of the bag in a sparkling shower.
The girls and Honey rushed to scoop up
the tiny, sweet-shaped sparkles – but the
goblin was already there, grabbing
great glittering handfuls.

"Just what Jack Frost wanted," he
gloated, stuffing it into his pockets.
"Now I've got this fairy dust, his party
will be better than ever!"

"Oh, no, it won't!" Kirsty shouted, grabbing a striped candy cane from the floor. Rachel did the same, and the two

girls started poking the goblin in the ribs with them. "Ooh! Ah! Tee hee..." the goblin giggled helplessly, as the canes tickled him. "Stop! Stop it!"

The goblin was laughing so hard that he lost his balance. He stumbled and skidded on the gobstoppers that were all over the floor. "Whoaaaa!" he cried, his arms flailing. And then, "OW!" he shouted, as he fell over.

All of the fairy dust bounced out
of his pockets as he landed and
began vanishing before
his eyes. The goblin
stretched out a gnarly
green hand to grab
it again, but Honey
was too quick for
him. She waved
her wand at the
candy canes and
muttered some
magical words.

Kirsty and Rachel
watched in delight as all
the candy canes on the floor
started to shimmer with a golden
glow. Then they leapt up and
marched smartly over to the goblin.

Before he could get his hands on any of
the vanishing fairy dust, the stripy
canes began herding him
across the room.
"Hey!" protested
the goblin, as the
canes pushed
him backwards.
"Stop that!"
But Honey's
magic was too
strong for him.
The grumbling
goblin was marched
right out of the back
door of the shop by
the dancing candy canes.
"That's got rid of him," Rachel laughed,
as the door swung shut behind the goblin.

"Phew," Honey sighed with relief, smiling at the girls. Then she fluttered down to look at her party bag, and the smile slipped from her face. "Oh, dear!" she cried. The fairy dust had all disappeared, and the bag was empty.

Kirsty glanced around the stockroom. It was a terrible mess. There were sweets all over the floor, and jars overturned on every shelf. "We'd better tidy this up before Mrs Twist sees it," she said anxiously. "It's going to take us ages."

"If only I had some fairy dust, I could magic everything to rights," Honey cried. "But that horrible goblin made me spill it all."

"Girls!" came Mrs Twist's voice from the shop. "Is everything all right in there?"

"Er, yes! We're just coming," Kirsty called back quickly. The girls looked at each other in panic. They could hear the shop bell jingling as yet more customers came in for sweets. What were they going to do?

A Flying Visit

Honey thought fast. "We'll have to go
to Fairyland and get new sweets," she
said. "I've made heaps for the jubilee
party – you can have some of those. And I
can refill my party bag with fairy dust, too."

Rachel bit her lip. "Do we have time?"
she asked. "Mrs Twist needs the sweets
right now."

"Don't worry," Honey assured her. "Once we've got the new sweets, I'll magic you both back here, and it'll be as if no time has passed at all."

"Brilliant!" Kirsty smiled. "What are we waiting for?"

Honey waved her wand over the girls, and amber sparkles swirled around them. There was a wonderful smell of spun sugar, and the girls felt themselves shrinking. The next thing they knew, they were whizzing through the air very fast.

"Here we are," came Honey's silvery voice a moment later. "Fairyland!"

Kirsty and Rachel blinked and looked round. They were the same size as Honey now – and best of all, they each had a pair of glittering fairy wings. Rachel beamed in delight and gave her wings a quick flutter.

Meanwhile, Kirsty was gazing at the magnificent golden castle that stood before them. Balloons and streamers fluttered from its towers, and jolly music floated from it on the breeze. There was the most delicious smell of baking in the air, too.

39

"Wow!" exclaimed Rachel. "Who lives here?"

"Nobody lives here," Honey giggled. "This is our Party Workshop."

Kirsty's eyes widened. "Bertram showed us some of the inside, but I never realised the outside looked so lovely," she said. "Still, I suppose we are in Fairyland. I should have known it would be gorgeous," she added happily.

Honey pushed open a golden gate. "This way," she called.

The girls followed her into the castle.

"This is Cherry's bakery," Honey told them, as they walked through a large, sunny kitchen.

Kirsty licked her lips. There were trays and trays of scrumptious chocolate cakes, strawberry tarts, cream sponges, blueberry muffins and lots more. Some fairies were carefully mixing ingredients, while others were icing the cakes with intricate jubilee designs.

"Look!" Rachel gasped suddenly. "There's the goblin who spoiled your birthday cake, Kirsty. I'd forgotten the Fairy Godmother had sent him here."

The girls watched as the goblin carefully piped pretty icing flowers onto a cake. "And to think he spent all that time spoiling cakes," Kirsty whispered to Rachel, "when actually, he's quite good at making them look beautiful!"

Cherry the Cake Fairy, fluttered over. "I thought it was you two," she smiled, pressing warm jam tarts into the girls' hands. "Try these. They're made from my new recipe, with fairy blackberries."

"Thank you," Kirsty replied, watching the fairy blackberries glitter with a magical purple light. They were so pretty, Kirsty thought, it was almost a shame to eat them.

"Yum," Rachel said, with her mouth full. "This is the most delicious jam tart I've ever tasted."

Kirsty took a bite and closed her eyes happily as the juicy, fairy blackberries popped sweetly in her mouth.

Then Honey led the girls through to another huge room, filled with brightly-coloured balloons. There were twinkling fairy lights strung all over the high, arched ceiling, and shining silver streamers twirling in mid-air.

But best of all was the fountain of glitter
in the middle of the room, which sparkled
in all the colours of the rainbow. Fairies
were collecting the glitter in pots, and
then stacking them to one side, while
Grace the Glitter Fairy fluttered about,
organising her helpers.

As soon as she saw the girls, she winked
and waved her wand at them, sending a
swirl of pink glitter shooting towards
them in a heart shape.

Rachel and Kirsty smiled and waved and then followed Honey through another door. They found themselves on a golden balcony, overlooking a magnificent hallway.

"We saw this bit when Bertram came to see us," Kirsty remembered. "Look, there's Melodie the Music Fairy – and the frog orchestra!"

It was wonderful to see so many frogs smartly dressed in red waistcoats and playing their musical instruments.

45

"There's Bertram," Rachel whispered, giving him a wave. Bertram was so excited to see the girls that he tooted his bugle in all the wrong places through "Happy Jubilee", as he tried to wave back.

Kirsty suddenly noticed that there was somebody else in the great hall too – the Fairy Godmother. The girls held their breath as she flew over to greet them.

"Hello again, girls," she smiled. "Have you and Honey been having goblin trouble, by any chance?"

"You could say that," Honey agreed, and she told the Fairy Godmother what had happened in Mrs Twist's sweet shop.

The Fairy Godmother chuckled. "Those wretched goblins!" she said. "Well, you'd better take Mrs Twist some magical sweets for her shop. That will make her customers happy again."

"Thank you," Kirsty breathed, her eyes shining.

The Fairy Godmother's eyes twinkled as she looked at the girls' happy faces.

Then she lifted her wand and waved it over their heads. "Fly, fairies, fly!" she said. "And keep up the good work."

Rachel was just about to reply, when she felt herself swept up in a warm, magical breeze. It lifted both girls off the ground and whisked them along through the air. The Fairy Godmother waved as they drifted away.

Honey laughed. She, too, was caught up in the gale. "It's a magical wind," she cried in delight. "A special fairy breeze that will take us to the Sweet Factory!"

The breeze whisked them along
the balcony and into another room,
where the girls recognised Jasmine
the Present Fairy. She was wrapping
up gifts in sparkling paper, with long,
looping ribbons that tied themselves
in perfect bows.

Rachel turned herself around with

her fairy wings so that she could watch Jasmine at work. "How do those ribbons do that?" she marvelled.

Jasmine smiled as the breeze took the girls past her. "Fairy dust," she replied, sprinkling some over a pretty pink ribbon. Immediately, the ribbon flew towards Rachel and tied itself neatly around her ponytail.

"Thank you!" Rachel called as the breeze swept her on.

In the next room, Phoebe the Fashion Fairy was hard at work, surrounded by rolls of glittering material, boxes of shiny sequins and rows of sparkling buttons that kept changing shape.

There were racks of gowns and outfits in every colour imaginable.

Phoebe called out a cheery hello – and the shining golden ballgown she was working on lifted an arm and waved, too!

Kirsty laughed and waved back. "This is the most exciting place in the world!" she declared. And then she gasped, and jumped in surprise, as the breeze carried them into a very busy room.

Fairies were dashing all over the place, trying to catch a shiny silver parcel with small pink wings that was zooming from ceiling to floor.

"This is Polly the Party Fun Fairy's room," Honey told the girls, as Polly flew over, smiling.

"This is my new game – Pass the Magic Parcel," Polly explained.

"What fun!" Rachel laughed.

But Kirsty yelped and ducked, because the mischievous parcel had come flying straight at her! She flapped her wings to get out of the way of the giggling fairies in pursuit.

"Bye, Polly," Honey called, catching Kirsty's hands and pulling her towards a pair of bright red doors. "It's my department next – the Sweet Factory," she announced proudly.

The breeze carried the girls and Honey through the doors and out into a sunlit courtyard. Then, just as suddenly as it had appeared, the magical wind died away, and the girls were set gently down on the ground again.

Honey immediately led them along
a path to a small orchard. Kirsty and
Rachel stared in wonder – the trees
seemed to be sparkling!

"Sugar frosting," Honey told them
with a grin. She broke off a handful of
glittering green leaves. "Here, try these."

Kirsty and Rachel bit into the sugared
leaves, which tasted deliciously of lime juice.

"Yummy!" Rachel declared, licking her lips.

"There are pear drops growing on these trees," Honey said, pointing. "And sherbet lemons over there." They all watched as a couple of fairies flew close to the trees, picking the sweets and putting them in golden baskets.

Further along, Rachel spotted some other fairies using great lengths of liquorice as skipping ropes. "What are they doing?" Rachel asked.

"Strength testing," Honey told her. "And making sure it's stretchy enough." She smiled. "Besides, liquorice makes the best skipping rope. You should try it sometime."

The next fairy they saw was making bon-bons bounce in and out of a huge jar of pink icing sugar. Fluffy, pink candy-floss flowers grew at her feet, while sugar mice ran about squeaking.

Honey filled up her party bag with
golden fairy dust from a frothing
sherbet fountain, then she took the
girls to her own stockroom. It was
piled high with boxes and jars of
fairy sweets. "Let's see... Fizzy
Fairies, Strawberry Sparkles,
Peppermint Pops, Chocolate
Bubbles..." Honey murmured,
loading boxes into the girls' arms.

"May we have some toffees too, please?" Kirsty asked, suddenly remembering the errand her mum had sent her on. It seemed a long time ago now.

"Of course!" Honey smiled. She waved her wand, and a jar of toffees appeared at the top of Kirsty's pile.

"Fantastic," Rachel beamed. "Now Mrs Twist is going to have a wonderful leaving party!"

Home Sweet Home

"Time for me to take you home to your own world," Honey said, once the girls were fully laden. She waved her wand again and Rachel and Kirsty found themselves surrounded by amber sparkles. Fairyland seemed to melt away before their eyes, there was a delicious smell of honey, a whirl of colours and then...

"Girls? Have you found the sweets?"
Mrs Twist was calling.

Honey, Rachel and Kirsty were
back in the stockroom of the sweet
shop. And the girls were back to their
normal size, too.

"Coming!" Kirsty called breathlessly.

"I'll just sort this mess out before
I go," Honey said, and she drew a
handful of fairy dust from her party
bag and threw it into the air. For a

moment, the whole stockroom glowed
with golden light – and then the fun
began! The jelly snakes started wiggling
their way back to their jar. The
gobstoppers bounced into *their* jar and
whizzed around inside it with a noisy
rattle, and the jelly babies hopped into
their box one by one.

As soon as all the jars and boxes were
full, they flew back onto their shelves
and lined themselves up neatly.

Kirsty realised her mouth was hanging open as she watched the fairy magic at work. "I wish I could borrow your fairy dust to tidy my bedroom," she joked. "Honey, that was brilliant!"

Honey gave a little curtsey in mid-air, then flew over to hug both girls goodbye. "I must go back to Fairyland, now," she said. "But thank you for saving me and my party bag from the goblin."

"And thank you for all these gorgeous sweets," Rachel replied.

"We'll see you again at the jubilee party," Kirsty added.

Honey looked serious for a moment.
"As long as those goblins don't mess
everything up," she said. "Goodbye!"
And with a final flourish of her wand
and a stream of
golden sparkles,
she was gone.

Kirsty breathed
in the smell of
honey, which was
all that remained of
their fairy friend. She
hated saying goodbye.

"Come on," Rachel said,
seeing Kirsty's wistful face.
"Let's take these to Mrs Twist."

The two girls staggered
through to the shop with all their
Fairyland goodies.

"Goodness, you have done well!" Mrs Twist exclaimed. "Now, let's see…" She peered at one of the jars. "Fizzing Fairies?" she read aloud. "I don't remember buying these." She unscrewed the lid to reveal lots of fairy-shaped sweets, all beautifully wrapped.

"Can I try one, please?" a little girl asked shyly.

"Of course," Mrs Twist beamed. She raised her eyebrows as she handed the jar around. "Don't they smell lovely? I think I'll try one myself."

Kirsty elbowed Rachel in delight. She was sure she'd just spotted the fairy on the label giving them both a wink. And as the girls looked closer, they realised that all of the Fizzing Fairies were in the shapes of their friends, the Party Fairies.

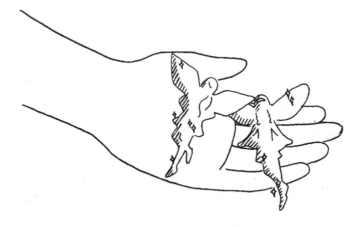

"Mmmmm," all the boys and girls said, licking their lips as Mrs Twist opened up more of the jubilee party sweets. "These are the best sweets ever!"

Kirsty and Rachel agreed. The marshmallows were soft and fluffy. The liquorice was stretchy and chewy. And the pear drops were scrumptiously tangy.

"Freshly picked this morning," Rachel joked in a low voice.

Kirsty felt something rustle in her pocket. She put her hand in to find a small bag of toffees, carefully tied with a curling gold ribbon. There was a sticker of a honey bee on the front of the bag. And on a label – in gold, shimmering writing – Kirsty read the words "Made with love and honey in Fairyland…"

"Wow," Kirsty breathed. "Look!" Then she smiled. "I think we'd better take these home before I start eating them. Don't they look delicious?"

The two friends said goodbye to
Mrs Twist and left the shop.

"Well, that was certainly the tastiest
trip to Fairyland yet," Rachel
commented.

Kirsty nodded happily. "Just three
days left until the jubilee party," she
said. "I can't wait!"

"I hope we get to play Pass the
Magic Parcel," Rachel added, laughing
as she remembered Polly's game.

Kirsty laughed, too. "One thing's for sure," she said, as she popped a final pear drop into her mouth, "we're definitely going to have sweet dreams tonight!"

The Party Fairies

Cherry, Melodie, Grace and Honey
have got their magic party bags back.
Now Rachel and Kirsty must help

Polly the Party Fun Fairy

Win a Rainbow Magic
Sparkly T-Shirt and Goody Bag!

In every book in the Rainbow Magic Party Fairies
series (books 15-21) there is a hidden picture of a magic
party bag with a secret letter in it. Find all seven letters
and re-arrange them to make a special Fairyland
word, then send it to us. Each month we will put the
entries into a draw and select one winner to receive a
Rainbow Magic Sparkly T-shirt and Goody Bag!

Send your entry on a postcard to Rainbow Magic
Competition, Orchard Books, 96 Leonard Street,
London EC2A 4XD. Australian readers should write
to Level 17/207 Kent St, Sydney, NSW 2000.
Don't forget to include your name and address.
Only one entry per child. Final draw: 28th April 2006.

Coming Soon...
The Jewel Fairies

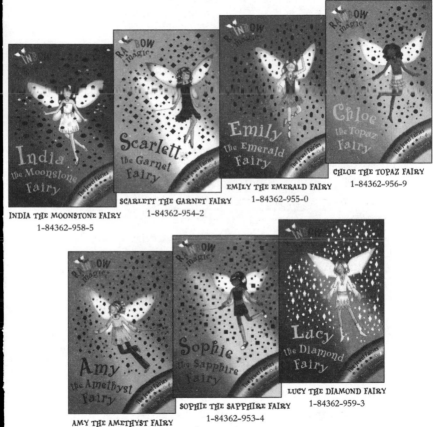

INDIA THE MOONSTONE FAIRY
1-84362-958-5

SCARLETT THE GARNET FAIRY
1-84362-954-2

EMILY THE EMERALD FAIRY
1-84362-955-0

CHLOE THE TOPAZ FAIRY
1-84362-956-9

AMY THE AMETHYST FAIRY
1-84362-957-7

SOPHIE THE SAPPHIRE FAIRY
1-84362-953-4

LUCY THE DIAMOND FAIRY
1-84362-959-3

Also coming soon . . .

SUMMER THE HOLIDAY FAIRY

1-84362-638-1

Summer the Holiday Fairy is getting all hot and bothered, trying to keep Rainspell Island the best place to go on vacation. Jack Frost has stolen the sand from the beaches, and three magical shells. The fairies need Rachel and Kirsty's help to get the holiday magic back...